Cousins of Clouds

Elephant Poems

BY **Tracie Vaughn Zimmer**

ILLUSTRATED BY

Megan Halsey AND **Sean Addy**

CLARION BOOKS

Houghton Mifflin Harcourt

New York • Boston • 2011

Cousins of Clouds

Long, long ago,
before man tamed words on the page
and when elephants
were great kings of the sky,
ruling the storms,
inking out the sun,
stampeding across the stars,
there was a great counselor and prophet
who traveled to the most remote mountain villages
to share all he knew.

As word spread of the master's visit,
many gathered under the arms
of an ancient elm,
and even a great flock of
elephants swooped in with
the first ribbons of dawn
to perch in the branches and listen.

But a quarrel erupted
among the elephants
over who had the best view,
causing the limbs of the tree
to fracture and fall,
crushing all but the prophet himself.

Furious,
the prophet invoked a dreadful curse,
shriveling the elephants' prized wings
into pitiful ears,
chaining the elephant
to gravity and man's will
for all eternity.

To this very day
you can see the poor elephants
flapping their ears,
dreaming of flight,
but now only
cousins of clouds.

Many cultures have assigned supernatural powers to elephants. The Mbuti people of Africa believed that the souls of their departed were carried around by elephants. The ancient Romans thought elephants were priests who worshiped the moon and stars. Others thought they controlled the weather and could even hurl lightning from their trunks.

Besides an elephant's trunk, its most distinguishing characteristic is its immense size. African elephants are almost twice the size of Asian elephants, which are actually a separate species. You can tell the difference between them by the shapes of their ears and heads (Asians have two humps, called domes, on their foreheads). Asian elephants weigh between 6,000 and 14,000 pounds, whereas African elephants can top out near 16,000 pounds (about the weight of a midsize car). African elephants are the largest mammals to walk the earth; only the blue whale is larger.

Landscape

An elephant's skin—
scored clay drying in the sun,
begging for soft rains.

Legs

Great pillars that hold
an elephant's massive bulk:
an architect's dream.

Accessory

Tapered rope of tail
swings as the elephant walks,
a fancy tassel.

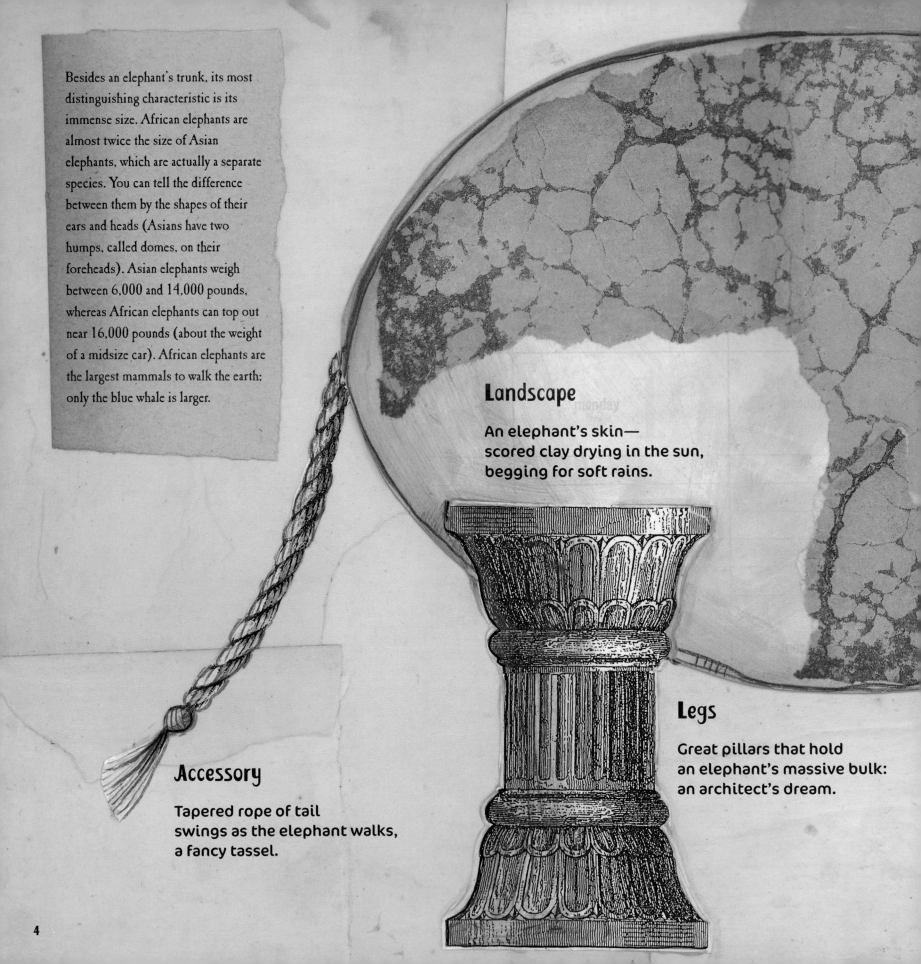

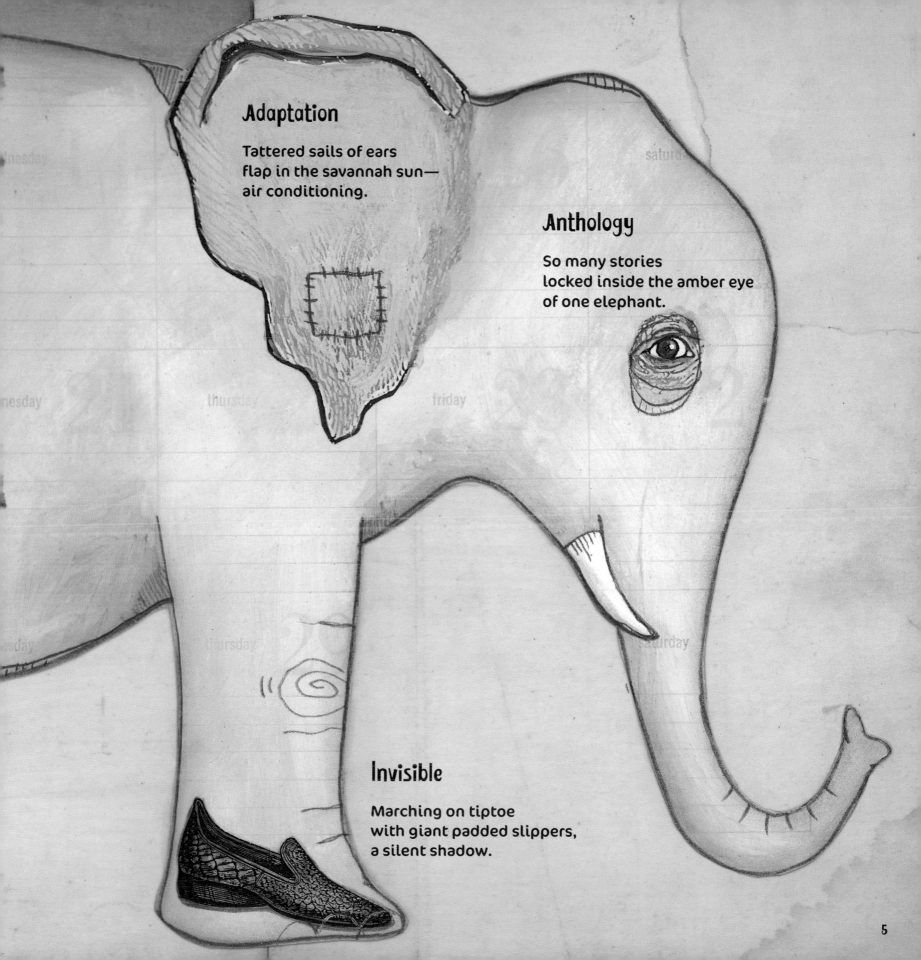

Adaptation

Tattered sails of ears
flap in the savannah sun—
air conditioning.

Anthology

So many stories
locked inside the amber eye
of one elephant.

Invisible

Marching on tiptoe
with giant padded slippers,
a silent shadow.

5

Beggars of Bangkok

I buy bananas
from the mahout riding his elephant
down the busy Bangkok street.
The cool, moist finger of the elephant's trunk,
as gentle as my grandmother's hands,
plucks my offering, and
the still green bananas disappear
in one gulp.

The mahout kicks the flesh
behind the tattered, speckled ears,
and the elephant turns—
diamonds of reflective tape
mark his giant hind
and swing on the metronome of his tail
so the cacophony of cars
will notice his shadowed form.

Out into this neon night,
the homeless giant
moves on.

Vantage

When I pat her head,
Jontu flails her trunk;
a low rumble vibrates through me as if
I'm an instrument she plays.
A tuft of her spiky hair prickles my knees,
and she flaps oven-hot air across me
with her wide, serrated ears.

Slowly, our parade of pachyderms
trails into the dappled light
to spy with a new vantage
the shy giraffes unfurling
their long purple tongues,
hippos soaking in muddy ponds,
a pride of lions lazing in midday sun.

Each step rocking me,
an African lullaby.

Asian elephants have been domesticated for hundreds of years to work in agriculture and logging industries. Since many of the ancient forests of Southeast Asia have been logged out, the elephants that worked those lands have become unemployed, along with their mahouts, or handlers. Quickly becoming a burden in small villages because of their voracious appetites, elephants live in empty lots or in city dumps and beg for food on the streets. The small profit mahouts make can support their families in rural villages. In Africa, elephants have also been recruited into the tourism industry, in part to help support local villages that lose crops to their pillaging. The relationship between these magnificent animals and the people who live near them is a complex one.

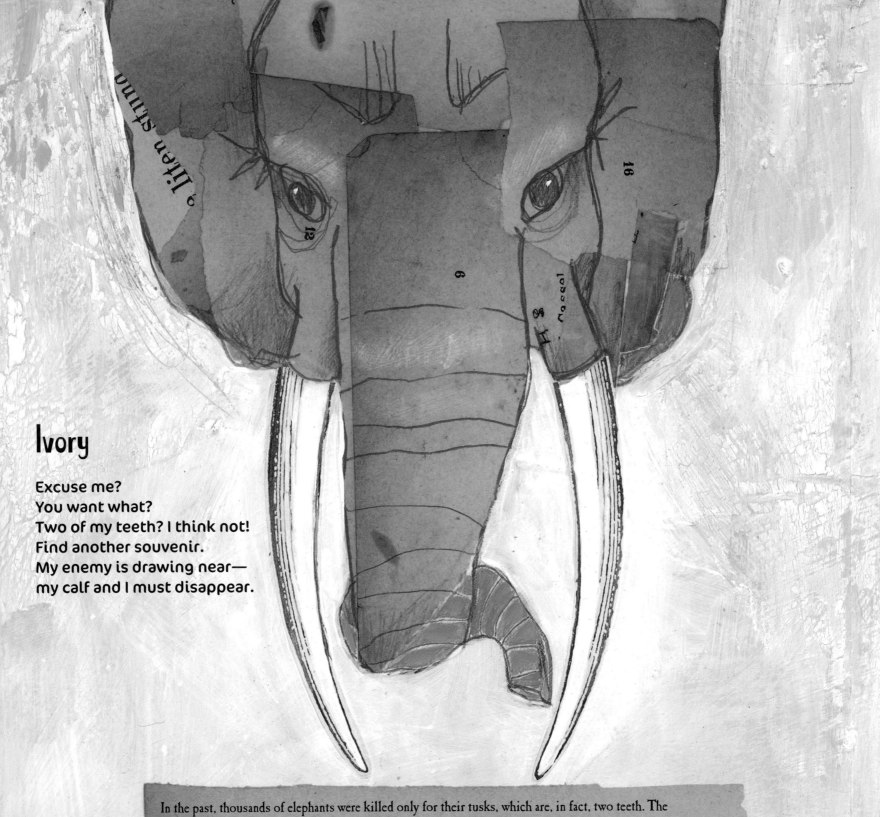

Ivory

Excuse me?
You want what?
Two of my teeth? I think not!
Find another souvenir.
My enemy is drawing near—
my calf and I must disappear.

In the past, thousands of elephants were killed only for their tusks, which are, in fact, two teeth. The population of elephants shrank greatly because of poaching, or illegal killing. In 1989, world leaders signed a boycott, or ban, on ivory. Since then, some countries have asked for permission to sell ivory collected from elephants that have died naturally so they can fund more environmental projects for elephants, but many believe that even a onetime lift of the ban will encourage the poachers to begin their destruction again.

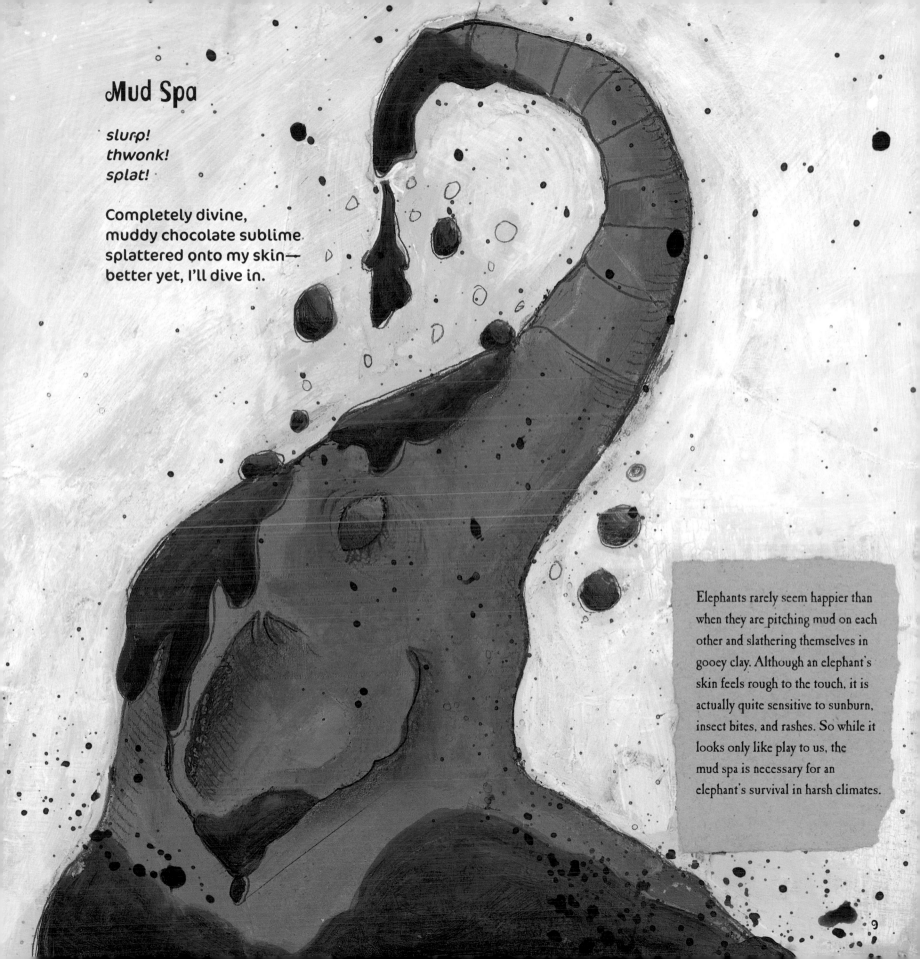

Mud Spa

slurp!
thwonk!
splat!

Completely divine,
muddy chocolate sublime.
splattered onto my skin—
better yet, I'll dive in.

Elephants rarely seem happier than when they are pitching mud on each other and slathering themselves in gooey clay. Although an elephant's skin feels rough to the touch, it is actually quite sensitive to sunburn, insect bites, and rashes. So while it looks only like play to us, the mud spa is necessary for an elephant's survival in harsh climates.

9

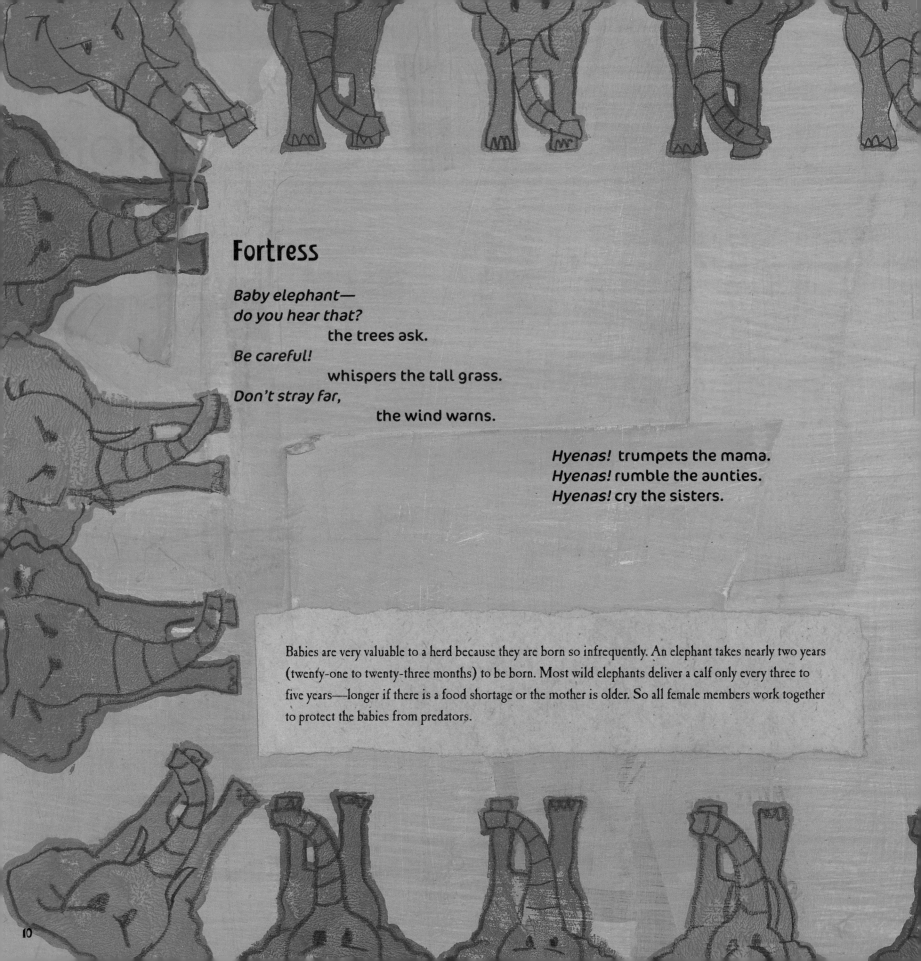

Fortress

Baby elephant—
do you hear that?
              the trees ask.
Be careful!
              whispers the tall grass.
Don't stray far,
              the wind warns.

                    Hyenas! trumpets the mama.
                    Hyenas! rumble the aunties.
                    Hyenas! cry the sisters.

Babies are very valuable to a herd because they are born so infrequently. An elephant takes nearly two years (twenty-one to twenty-three months) to be born. Most wild elephants deliver a calf only every three to five years—longer if there is a food shortage or the mother is older. So all female members work together to protect the babies from predators.

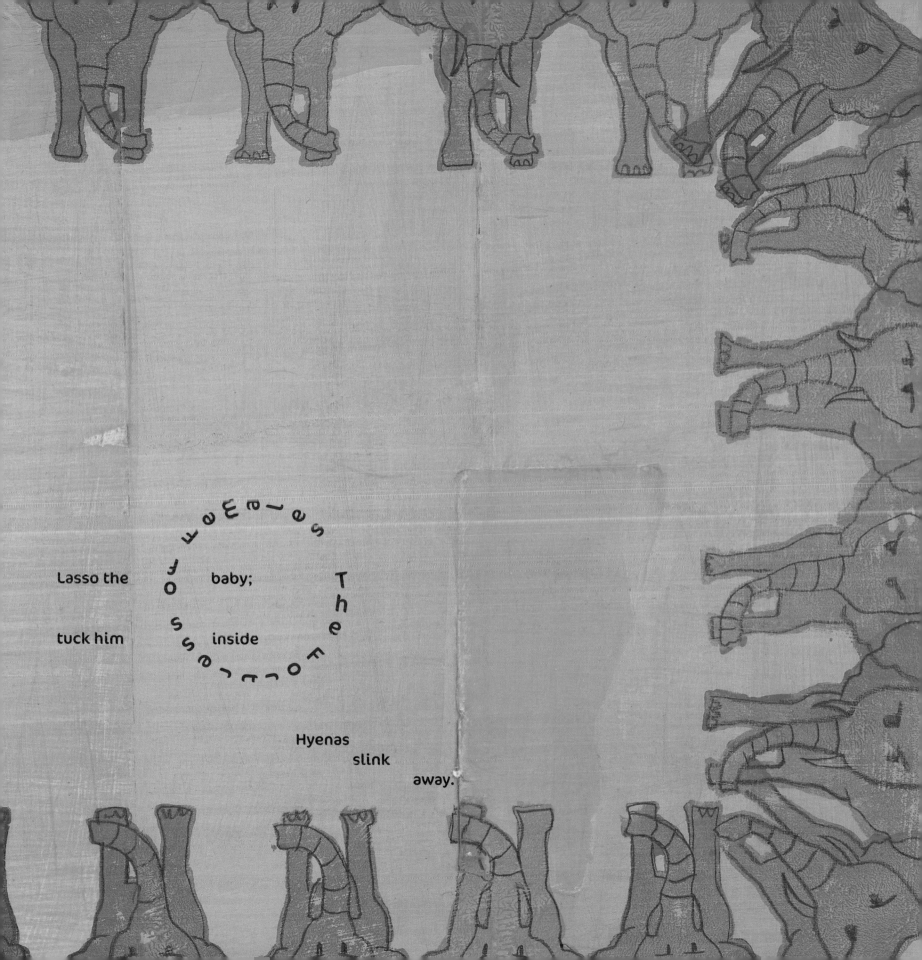

Lasso the baby;

tuck him inside

The Forgetfulness of the Forest

Hyenas slink away.

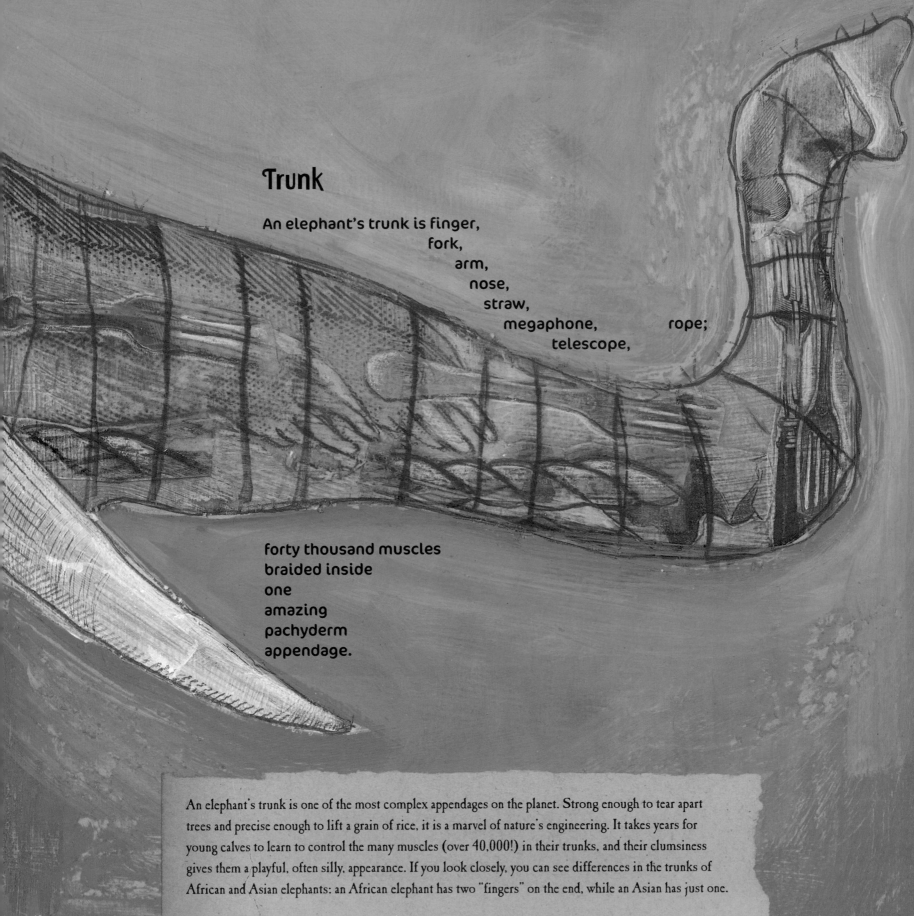

Trunk

An elephant's trunk is finger,
fork,
arm,
nose,
straw,
megaphone,   rope;
telescope,

forty thousand muscles
braided inside
one
amazing
pachyderm
appendage.

An elephant's trunk is one of the most complex appendages on the planet. Strong enough to tear apart trees and precise enough to lift a grain of rice, it is a marvel of nature's engineering. It takes years for young calves to learn to control the many muscles (over 40,000!) in their trunks, and their clumsiness gives them a playful, often silly, appearance. If you look closely, you can see differences in the trunks of African and Asian elephants: an African elephant has two "fingers" on the end, while an Asian has just one.

White Elephant

I am
the sacred white
elephant of Thailand.
Give me offerings worthy of
a king.

Tempt me
with your best foods;
I am your honored guest.
And expect no help with your chores
from me.

Or I
will curse your home
with famine and disease,
bankrupt you with my appetite—
no gift.

Have you ever heard someone say they were given a "white elephant"? This expression means the person received a gift that no one else would want. The term refers to the rare white elephant of Southeast Asia, which is considered sacred and is highly prized. Because of its special status in the culture, it must be treated in a very specific, very expensive way. In the past, when one kingdom gave a white elephant to another, it was a token of friendship and peace. A king who had one in his care was expected to have a long and prosperous reign. However, if he failed to treat the white elephant as his honored guest, he (and his people) would be cursed!

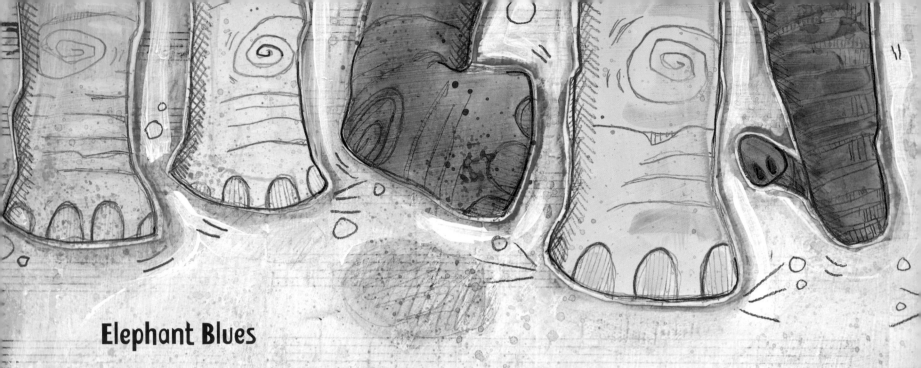

Elephant Blues

In the bright daylight under the African sun,
I say, when the sun is bright in the African light,
I call to my brethren across the miles,
singing the elephant's plight—
do you know the elephant's plight?

If a quake rattles the earth out of her sleep,
if the earth shivers and shakes way down deep,
I'll feel the warning through my sensitive feet
and flee for highest ground,
follow me to the highest ground.

When the day disappears into the arms of night,
when the sky starts to smear in the dappled light,
I'll make the call to find a new site—
fresh shoots in a watering hole,
we've got to find a new watering hole.

The study of elephant communication is one of the fastest-growing segments of research about
these fascinating animals. Scientists only recently discovered that not only are elephants able to
communicate over extremely long distances with sounds too low for the naked human ear to

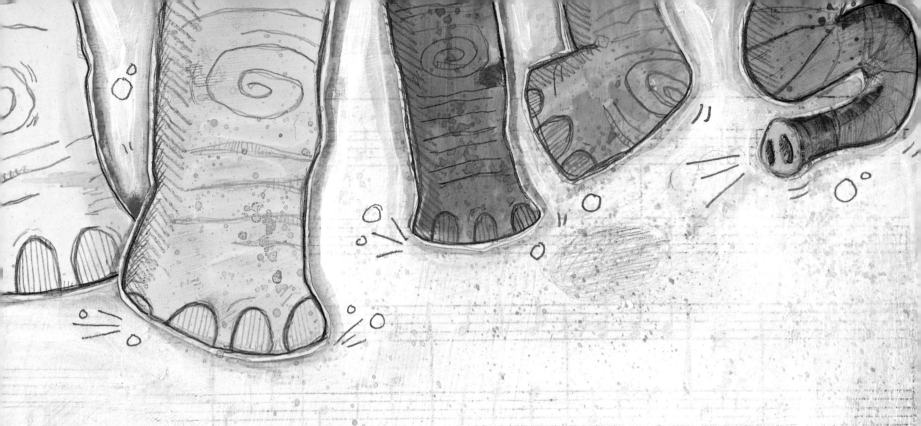

When the low-down lion stalks our young and sick,
oh, I say, if the lion slinks around with his terrible tricks,
I'll send out messages
near silent but quick—
run, my sisters, run!

If the days have piled up since my family has met,
too many moons crossed my head since my family last met,
then we'll trumpet and sing
as loud as we can get
when we see each other again.

Oh, yes, when we see each other again.

hear (called infrasound), but they can actually feel the tones through their very sensitive feet!
This is why elephants in Thailand became agitated and ran for higher ground before the 2004
tsunami even reached land, saving themselves and the tourists lucky enough to be on their backs.

Orphan

The baby elephant
wraps the arm of
her trunk
around her foster mama,
a Kenyan boy.

Umbrella

Imagine keeping
a tumbling, wrestling,
frolicking baby elephant
under the shade
of one umbrella.

On the outskirts of Nairobi, Kenya, there is a remarkable orphanage and hospital. Baby elephants that are orphaned by accident, injury, or poachers are brought to the David Sheldrick Wildlife Trust. Orphans receive round-the-clock care from their devoted keepers until they are healed and learn the survival skills they need to be released into the wild inside the Tsavo National Park.

Dear Lola,

Are you bored

by the toys

in your yard, like me?

Do you wish

to unlatch the tall gate

and escape?

Would you chase the zebras?

Play tag with the giraffes?

Throw water balloons at the ostriches

so they'd pick up their fluffy feathered gowns

and run on the high heels of their pink feet?

Would you?

Me too.

Your friend,

Grounded Too

Although zoo elephants lack freedom and mobility, at least they aren't threatened by poachers or starvation. Many animal activists have worked to make captive elephants' living conditions less harsh. It is now considered cruel, for example, to house an elephant without others of its kind. And many zoos offer their elephants diversions such as painting, training, and games to keep them stimulated and entertained.

This Is Just to Say
(for Jumbo)

I have offered
you treats
laced
with medicine,

and which
you probably
never expected
from me.

Forgive me;
they were bitter,
but it was
for your own good.

An elephant's memory can be as long as its life span (more than sixty years).
They are often slow to forgive those who have deceived or mistreated them.
One trainer reported that after he tricked his charge into swallowing a bitter
medicine, the elephant never missed a chance to trumpet in his ear, and
stomped a warning whenever he saw the trainer approach. There have also
been reports of a few aggressive elephants that have sought revenge against
trainers who used cruel methods against them.

Grace

The elephants line up
like kindergartners
before recess:
trunk to tail,
twelve in a row,
waiting for the ringmaster's cue
to begin the parade
around the ring.

The first elephant carries
a woman in a beaded costume,
perched on a silk-embroidered saddle
thrown over the crisscrossed
map of its skin.

After discovering a popcorn bucket
with a few stray kernels inside,
the elephant squashes it—
making the giant bracelet of bells
ting
ting
ting
around its ankle.

The jewels around the elephant's face
flash in the colored lights,
but the ginger jewel of her eye
haunts me,
even in sleep.

Elephants have been used for public exhibition as far back as 1000 B.C. in India. Romans would capture elephants on expeditions in Africa and ship them home to the coliseum to fight gladiators and slaves in front of vast crowds; often hundreds would be destroyed in a single event. These days, elephants are no longer allowed to be imported, so circus owners must ensure that a new generation of elephant entertainers is continually born.

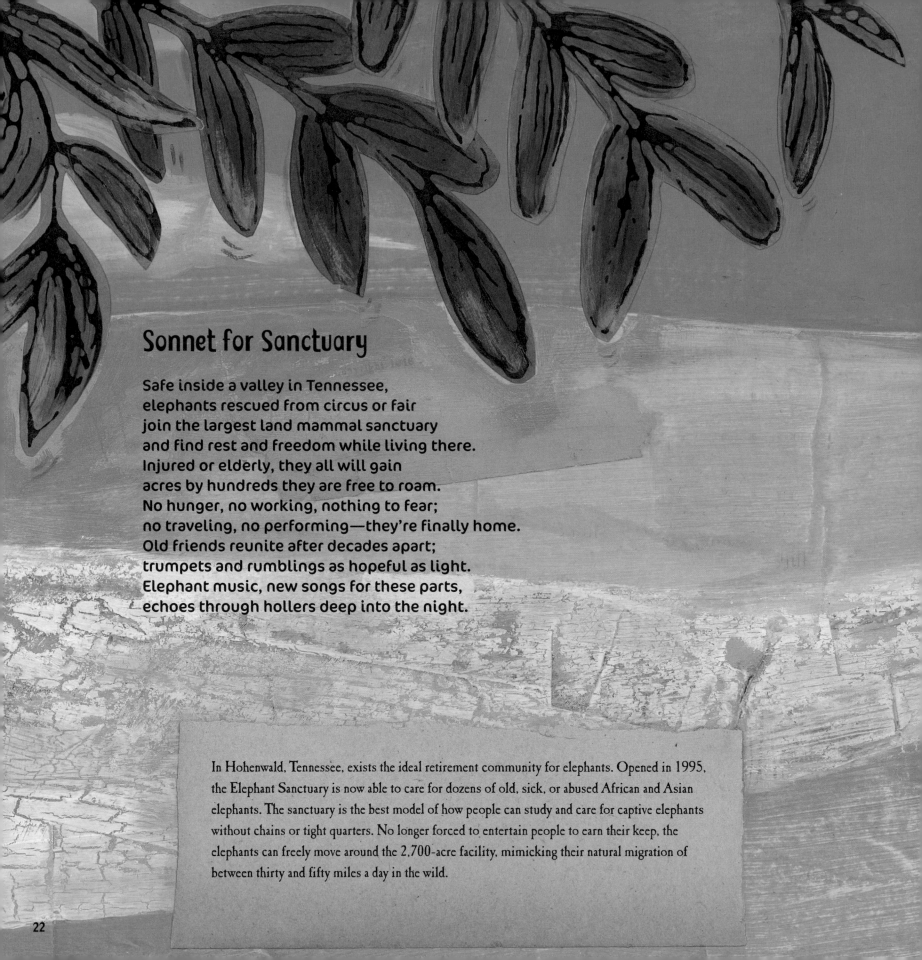

Sonnet for Sanctuary

Safe inside a valley in Tennessee,
elephants rescued from circus or fair
join the largest land mammal sanctuary
and find rest and freedom while living there.
Injured or elderly, they all will gain
acres by hundreds they are free to roam.
No hunger, no working, nothing to fear;
no traveling, no performing—they're finally home.
Old friends reunite after decades apart;
trumpets and rumblings as hopeful as light.
Elephant music, new songs for these parts,
echoes through hollers deep into the night.

In Hohenwald, Tennessee, exists the ideal retirement community for elephants. Opened in 1995, the Elephant Sanctuary is now able to care for dozens of old, sick, or abused African and Asian elephants. The sanctuary is the best model of how people can study and care for captive elephants without chains or tight quarters. No longer forced to entertain people to earn their keep, the elephants can freely move around the 2,700-acre facility, mimicking their natural migration of between thirty and fifty miles a day in the wild.

A Riddle

I am the Hindu god of beginnings.
My head is the wise elephant's
but my body, a rotund man's.
I have four hands and one tusk,
and I ride a mouse.

I am the patron of scientists,
merchants, writers, and thieves.
The wise Hindu
who hopes to succeed
leaves me offerings
before journeys
of body, mind, or spirit.

Do you know my name?

Answer: Ganesh

The son of the gods Shiva and Parvati, Ganesh is one of the most
revered and beloved gods of the Hindu religion. His image and
temples are found throughout India.

Patience

The elephant soaks her nomadic feet
in the lapping waves,
and the sticky mud feels
cool against her bulk.
She siphons water with her trunk
and sprays
misty droplets
on her head.

The baby
clambers
on the ledge of her knee,
steps on tender ears,
thin skin of eye,
yet she never scolds him;
instead she
nuzzles under his chin,
rinses his cheek
with her gentle trunk.

This baby elephant,
bathed
in mother love.

In general, elephants make terrific mothers. Most are infinitely
patient and gentle with their beloved babes. Calves often nurse for
several years and are almost always within reach of their mother's
trunk. Females live their entire lives within the same family they
were born into. The matriarch, the oldest of the female elephants,
leads the herd.

Memory

She detours through brush
to caress the sun-bleached bones
of her lost sister.

Elephants seem to experience life with as much emotion as humans do; perhaps this is why people have long been fascinated by them. When reuniting with relatives, they have an elaborate celebration in which they trumpet and embrace with their trunks. Like us, elephants grieve when a family member dies, and they will often visit the bones of a family member even dozens of years after a death.

Elephants from around the world!

Inspiration

An elephant's image,

carved on tombs
interred with pharaohs,

hewn in stone,
guarding India's palaces,

laid in tile
for Istanbul's king,

sculpted to size
on China's Avenue of Spirits,

illustrated in texts
for medieval scholars,

woven into masks
for Africa's secret societies,

etched in the imagination
of all mankind,

a behemoth of hope.

Ancient Egypt

India

India

Istanbul, Turkey

No matter where you might travel in the world, you're likely to encounter art that features elephants. Even where they have never been native to the landscape, they have inspired artists and poets for millennia.

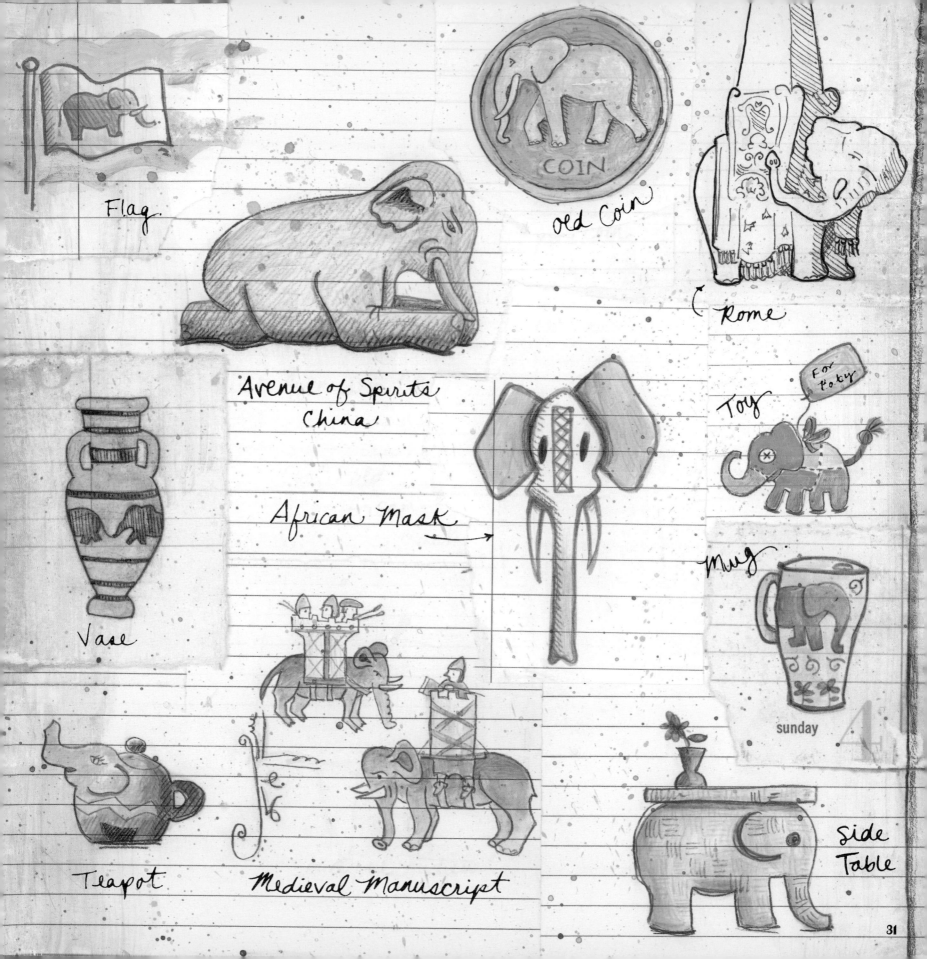

Flag.

old Coin

Rome

Avenue of Spirits
China

African Mask

Toy

For Toby

Mug

Vase

sunday 4

Teapot

Medieval Manuscript

Side Table

31

For further elephant reading

Coming of Age with Elephants: A Memoir by Joyce Poole (Hyperion Books, 1997)

Elephant Memories: Thirteen Years in the Life of an Elephant Family
by Cynthia Moss (University of Chicago Press, 2000)

The Elephant's Secret Sense: The Hidden Life of the Wild Herds of Africa
by Caitlin O'Connell (University of Chicago Press, 2008)

In friendship and creative fellowship, to
Jessica Swaim and Julia Durango—T.V.Z.

With thanks to Eric Duning, elephant keeper,
and the Cincinnati Zoo.

For my friend, who feels like family, Ginny—M.H.

For my mother-in-law, Joan, for all her hard work
and dedication to her family—S.A.

Clarion Books
215 Park Avenue South, New York, New York 10003
Text copyright © 2011 by Tracie Vaughn Zimmer
Illustrations copyright © 2011 by Megan Halsey and Sean Addy

The illustrations were executed in mixed media collage.
The text was set in 12-point Cocon.

Clarion Books is an imprint of Houghton Mifflin Harcourt Publishing Company.

www.hmhbooks.com

Manufactured in China

Library of Congress Cataloging-in-Publication Data

Zimmer, Tracie Vaughn.
Cousins of clouds : elephant poems / by Tracie Vaughn Zimmer ; illustrated by Megan Halsey and Sean Addy.
p. cm.
Facts about elephants interspersed with poems.   ISBN 978-0-618-90349-8
1. Elephants—Juvenile literature. 2. Elephants—Juvenile poetry. 3. Elephants in art. I. Halsey, Megan, ill.
II. Addy, Sean, ill. III. Title. IV. Title: Elephant poems.

QL737.P98Z563 2010   599.67—dc22

2009030226

LEO   10   9   8   7   6   5   4   3   2   1

4500260434